What the Snakes Wrote

Hazel Hutchins
Art by Tina Holdcroft

annick press
toronto + new york + vancouver

It was Rufus who first noticed the snakes.
They were lying on the dirt in front of his
doghouse. They were alive and healthy.

But their bodies were curled and twisted
in ways that were very strange for snakes.

The shapes seemed somehow familiar.

Rufus set out on farmyard patrol. Fall harvest was over. The farmer was in a far corner of the land, checking out a hole he'd found while clearing brush the day before.

Snakes in trouble

The pigs were wallowing.
The cows were content.
The horse was happy.

But here, again, more snakes had
twisted themselves in unusual ways.

As Rufus crossed the road to the sheep pasture,
he saw something horrible about to happen!

Rufus herded the snakes to safety just in time.

The snakes disappeared into the grass, instantly camouflaged. Whatever they had been up to, they seemed to have lost interest. Things were back to normal. Rufus checked the sheep and headed to the farmhouse for a nap.

But things were not normal at all. The snakes had moved out of the grass again and into another open space.

Rufus thought, they must want to be seen! They were curling and twisting. And more were arriving. More and more and more.

Dog. Please help. Snakes in trouble. Need

Rufus had no idea what was going on, but it was time to get the farmer.

"Hello there, Rufus," said the farmer. "Feeling lonely?"

Rufus tugged at the farmer's jeans. "Sorry, I can't play now," said the farmer. "This hole is deep and dangerous. It might be an old well. I've just barely started to fill it in."

Rufus rolled over and raced in circles.
"Exactly," said the farmer. "Someone
might tumble down. Or a horse might
break its leg."

Rufus howled in frustration. "Rufus, are you hurt?" asked the farmer.

Rufus pretended his front paw was injured. He hobbled—just out of the farmer's reach—all the way back to the farmhouse. It took so long that by the time they got there, things had fallen apart.

One snake had swallowed something large.
Another was finding it hard to hold its loop.
Young snakes were chasing grasshoppers.
An older snake was shedding its skin. And
another had been carried away entirely.

The farmer checked Rufus's paw. "There's a burr between the pads of your foot," he said. "There, all cleaned out." The farmer headed back to the field.

"Lots of garter snakes around," he called over his shoulder. "They always seem to show up in greater numbers in the spring and fall. They're harmless to you and me, Rufus. Still, they usually stay more hidden."

The farmer hadn't seen what was really happening.
Rufus and the snakes were disappointed.

The snakes began to curl and twist
with new determination. Rufus
could tell this was important.

He streaked like the wind across the field,

grabbed the shovel from the farmer's
hands, and took off again.

"Rufus! Come back!" called
the farmer, chasing him.

Rufus raced up the steps. The farmer's
eyes grew round with amazement. He
read the words aloud.

"That arrow points right toward the hole I was planning to fill in," he added. "Good dog, Rufus. I'd have missed their message without you." Rufus wagged his tail.

"Let me know if they write anything else," said the farmer. "I need to do some research."

Rufus kept his eyes on the snakes. He kept his ears on the farmer. He heard the farmer taking books from the shelves, turning on the computer, and talking on the telephone.

"That's it!" called the farmer.
"I think I've got just what I need."

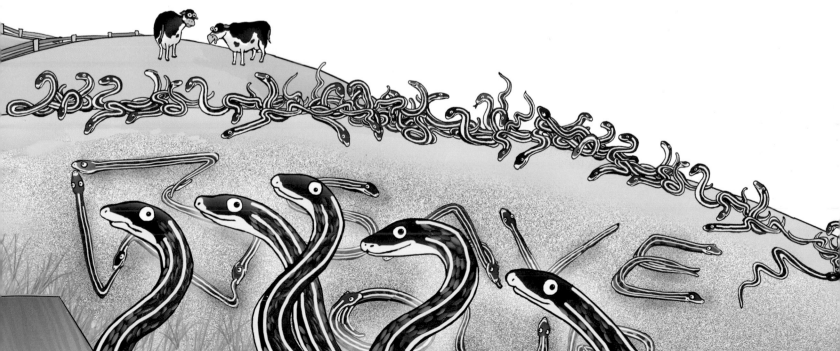

"In cold weather, snakes are in danger of freezing to death," the farmer explained. "But staying in a deep hole below the frosty ground saves them. It never gets cold enough to freeze down there. It's their winter den, Rufus!"

And so the hole was not filled with dirt. The farmer put a fence around it instead. People and farm animals were kept safely away. Snakes could come and go as they pleased.

And that day at sunset, the snakes wrote the very best message of all.

Of course, snakes can't write!

But if they could, they might tell you that:

- In cold weather, even if snakes had fur, feathers, or parkas, they wouldn't stay warm. Snakes can't produce their own body heat. Mammals and birds can turn food energy into heat but snakes' body temperatures change with their surroundings. A place that doesn't freeze is important to snakes!

- The scientific name for a snake's winter den is *hibernaculum*. It can house tens, hundreds, or even thousands of snakes. Dens are used over and over, for many generations. Snakes also use smaller places, such as animal burrows. Sometimes they snuggle into openings along the outside of heated buildings.

- In spring, garter snakes like the ones in this book (okay, not quite like the ones in this book!) travel up to 32 km (20 miles) from their den to spend the warm weather feeding and reproducing in woodlands, pastures, and other snake-friendly habitats. When fall arrives, they head back to the den for the winter.

- When a snake sticks out its tongue, it's not being rude. Its forked tongue picks up tiny particles from the air. The tips of the tongue are then quickly placed into pits in the roof of its mouth. This is part of how a snake's sense of smell works.

- A snake doesn't have to open its mouth to stick out its tongue, either. Its tongue can flick in and out through a small notch at the front of its mouth.

- Your parents would not like snakes' table manners! They eat their food whole. They never chew. Their food is often larger than their head. This is possible because snakes' jaws can unhinge and their skin can stretch. They can also stop breathing for periods of time while swallowing.

- Don't expect snakes to blink, wink, or close their eyes. They can't. They don't have eyelids. A single clear scale protects the eye. It's called a *brille* and works a bit like goggles. When the snake sheds its skin, the brille is shed, too.

- A snake sheds its skin the way you might peel off a sock—if the sock reached right up to your head! The skin splits at the nose. As the snake moves, the skin turns inside out and rolls off backward. When the shedding is complete, the tail of the old skin points in the direction the snake was traveling.

- Some people don't like snakes because they aren't soft and fuzzy. In truth, large snakes often *eat* things that are soft and fuzzy! However, snakes, like all creatures, are part of the fascinating balance of the natural world.

Hurrah for snakes!

With gratitude to Dr. Anthony P. Russell, of the University of Calgary, for valuable advice on the facts about snakes.

Annick Press Ltd.

We acknowledge the support of the Canada Council for the Arts, the Ontario Arts Council, and the Government of Canada through the Canada Book Fund (CBF) for our publishing activities.

ONTARIO ARTS COUNCIL
CONSEIL DES ARTS DE L'ONTARIO

Cataloging in Publication

Hutchins, H. J. (Hazel J.)
    What the snakes wrote / Hazel Hutchins ; art by Tina Holdcroft.

Also issued in electronic format.
ISBN 978-1-55451-473-1 (bound).—ISBN 978-1-55451-472-4 (pbk.)

    1. Snakes—Juvenile fiction. I. Holdcroft, Tina II. Title.

PS8565.U826W43 2013   jC813'.54   C2012-906001-1

Distributed in Canada by:

Firefly Books Ltd.
66 Leek Crescent
Richmond Hill, ON L4B 1H1

Published in the U.S.A. by Annick Press (U.S.) Ltd.
Distributed in the U.S.A. by:
Firefly Books (U.S.) Inc.
P.O. Box 1338
Ellicott Station
Buffalo, NY 14205

Printed in China

Visit us at: www.annickpress.com
Visit Hazel Hutchins at: www.hazelhutchins.net
Visit Tina Holdcroft at: www.tinaholdcroft.com

for Alexander, Noah, and Luke
—H.H.

for Tom Morgan
—T.H.